P9-DEH-958

Pinny
in
Fall

~

JOANNE SCHWARTZ

ISABELLE MALENFANT

(g)

GROUNDWOOD BOOKS
HOUSE OF ANANSI PRESS
TORONTO   BERKELEY

Peachtree

Text copyright © 2018 by Joanne Schwartz
Illustrations copyright © 2018 by Isabelle Malenfant
Published in Canada and the USA in 2018 by Groundwood Books

All rights reserved. No part of this publication may be reproduced,
stored in a retrieval system or transmitted, in any form or by any
means, without the prior written consent of the publisher or a
license from The Canadian Copyright Licensing Agency
(Access Copyright). For an Access Copyright License, visit
www.accesscopyright.ca or call toll free to 1-800-893-5777.

Groundwood Books / House of Anansi Press
groundwoodbooks.com

We acknowledge for their financial support of our publishing
program the Canada Council for the Arts, the Ontario Arts
Council and the Government of Canada.

Canada Council   Conseil des Arts
for the Arts   du Canada

ONTARIO ARTS COUNCIL
CONSEIL DES ARTS DE L'ONTARIO
an Ontario government agency
un organisme du gouvernement de l'Ontario

With the participation of the Government of Canada
Avec la participation du gouvernement du Canada | Canadä

Library and Archives Canada Cataloguing in Publication
Schwartz, Joanne (Joanne F.), author
Pinny in fall / Joanne Schwartz ; illustrated by Isabelle
Malenfant.
Issued in print and electronic formats.
ISBN 978-1-77306-106-1 (hardcover). —
ISBN 978-1-77306-107-8 (PDF)
I. Malenfant, Isabelle, illustrator II. Title.
PS8637.C592P55 2018   jC813'.6   C2017-907511-X
C2017-907512-8

The illustrations were done with soft pastel, graphite pencil,
Q-tips and an electric eraser.
Design by Michael Solomon
Printed and bound in Malaysia

FSC
www.fsc.org
MIX
Paper from
responsible sources
FSC® C012700

In memory of Sheila Barry,
wise editor and fellow Maritimer,
with gratitude. — JS

In memory of Sheila Barry.
A brilliant publisher,
a wonderful person. — IM

A Chilly Morning

Pinny woke up feeling a little chilly. Her blanket had fallen off during the night, and there was a cool breeze coming through the window. All week she had felt the air getting colder, little by little, day by day.

To warm up, Pinny did her morning exercises. She spread her arms out and twisted her body from one side to another. She bent down and touched her toes. She lay on her back and stretched her legs over her head. Back and forth, up and down, over and over.

When she was all finished, Pinny stood up tall, took a deep breath and said, "Ah …"

The sky was brighter now. Pinny opened her door and stepped outside. The sun was peeking in and out of the clouds.

"What a funny day," said Pinny. "I don't know if it's going to rain or be sunny."

One thing was certain, though. Pinny was going for a walk.

Pinny packed a small bag. She put in a sweater in case it got cold, a rain hat in case it started raining, an apple and some cookies in case she got hungry, and her book in case she wanted to sit down on a comfy rock and read. She was ready to go.

As she started out the door, Pinny realized she had forgotten to take the most important thing of all — her treasure pouch. She liked to have it with her, just in case she found something special. It was hanging on a hook by the door. Pinny took it down and stuffed it into her bag. Then off she went.

Wind and Fog

$\mathcal{P}$inny tramped across the field. The grass had been growing all summer. Now it was so high it came up to Pinny's waist. The wind picked up and the grass waved this way and that, making a *shrr-shrr* sound. All around, the leaves were turning colors. The world looked dark red, faded yellow, dusty rose and bright gold.

"Hey, Pinny!" There were her friends Annie and Lou. "Where are you going?"

"I'm going to Lighthouse Point. Want to come along?"

"Yes, let's go!"

The three friends ran up the rocky, winding path toward the lighthouse. It was so windy at the top of the hill that Pinny's hair blew sideways. The lighthouse keeper waved to Pinny and Annie and Lou from the deck of the lighthouse.

"Come on," yelled Pinny. "Let's play tag." They scattered across the hill like leaves blowing in the wind.

Pinny chased Annie until she caught her. "You're it now."

Then Annie chased Lou until she caught him, and then Lou chased Pinny. Pinny ran until she was laughing so much that she fell down. Lou bumped into her, and Annie came up behind and landed on them both.

"Look out there," said Pinny. She pointed to a ship sailing just off the coast. The three friends settled down on a clump of rocks to watch the ship go by. Pinny shared her apple and cookies with Annie and Lou. Big waves crashed against the rocky shoreline, sending spray high into the air.

Pinny decided to share her book, too. It was a book of poems, and she and Annie and Lou took turns reading out loud, shouting poetry into the wind. The sun slipped behind the clouds once, twice, and then it was completely gone.

The Lighthouse

"There's fog rolling in toward the shore," said Pinny. "I can feel it in the air."

And just like that, the fog did roll in like a blanket, and everything turned misty white.

"Oh no," said Pinny. "The ship is too close to shore!"

Through the thick fog they heard a voice calling, "Pinny, Annie and Lou!"

"It's the lighthouse keeper," said Pinny. "Let's go!" They ran to the lighthouse as fast as they could. The lighthouse keeper met them at the little side door, and they all raced up the stairs.

"My helper is away today," he said. "I need some extra hands. We have to hurry! Pinny, you press the big red button to sound the foghorn. Annie and Lou, press the big yellow button to turn on the light."

The foghorn bellowed, the light turned around, and the fog got thicker and thicker.

Now there was nothing to do but wait. They went out on the deck and peered into the mist. They couldn't see a thing, and all they could hear above the bellows of the foghorn were the seagulls screeching loudly.

And then, just as suddenly as it had appeared, the fog was blown away by a strong wind, and behind it a big blue sky opened up.

Now they could see that the ship was heading out to sea, far away from the rocky shoreline. Pinny and Annie and Lou jumped up and down.

"Hooray, we saved the ship!"

The lighthouse keeper was very happy, too, and gave them each a piece of beach glass for all their help. Pinny's piece was shiny blue, and she dropped it into her treasure pouch for safekeeping.

A Special Kind of Rain

By the time Pinny got home, she was ready for a steamy cup of hot chocolate. She warmed up some milk and stirred in cocoa and sugar. When the cocoa was nice and hot, Pinny poured it into a mug. She carried it to her favorite chair by the window and sat down.

Pinny was picking up her book to read when she noticed something outside. Flashes of red, yellow and gold were flying past the window. It was raining leaves! Pinny thought she had never seen anything so beautiful.

Well, thought Pinny, *if it's raining I better get my rain hat and go outside.* Out she went and stood in the wind with leaves raining down all around her. They floated by this way and that, and landed in a pile at her feet.

Pinny walked about kicking leaves until she felt the chilly evening air making goose bumps on her arms.

She went inside, took off her rain hat and fished the sweater out of her bag. The bag was almost empty now. She had shared her apple and cookies with Annie and Lou, she had read her book out loud to the wind, she had used her rain hat for the raining leaves, and now she had her sweater on for the cool evening.

The only thing left in the bag was her little treasure pouch. And in her little treasure pouch was the piece of blue beach glass the lighthouse keeper had given her.

The light was fading, and the shady night
sky was growing dark. Pinny put her blue beach
glass on the window sill. The glass had been
washed so smooth by the ocean, it glowed in the
twilight like a tiny beacon of light.

DISCARDED

DISCARDED

J PICTURE SCHWARTZ
Schwartz, Joanne
Pinny in fall /
R2004989766 PTREE

Peachtree

Atlanta-Fulton Public Library